MARCELLA'S HOUSE

PLAYHOUSE

TOOL
SHED

PLAYROOM

This book belongs to:

_____

Raggedy Ann & Andy's

GROW
AND
LEARN
LIBRARY

VOLUME 4

RAGGEDY DOG
TO THE RESCUE!

A LYNX BOOK

This book is published by Lynx Books, a division of Lynx Communications, Inc., 41 Madison Avenue, New York, New York 10010. The name ''Lynx'' together with the logotype consisting of a stylized head of a lynx is a trademark of Lynx Communications, Inc.

Raggedy Ann and Andy's Grow-and-Learn Library, the names and depictions of Raggedy Ann, Raggedy Andy and all related characters are trademarks of Macmillan, Inc.

Marcella came into the playroom and looked around. She looked on the shelf. She looked in the toy box. Then she looked right at Raggedy Dog's bed. Raggedy Dog was sure that Marcella had come to take him to the park.

But it was Raggedy Cat that Marcella had come to get. Raggedy Dog watched as Marcella picked up Raggedy Cat and gave her a little hug.

And he watched as Marcella came back hours later, still cuddling Raggedy Cat close to her.

"You're so cute," Marcella cooed. "You were the cutest little kitten in the whole park," she said.

For a second, Raggedy Dog thought he actually heard Raggedy Cat purring out loud. Why is Marcella paying so much attention to *her*, he wondered. Raggedy Dog almost felt like snorting right out loud.

After Marcella left the playroom, Babette the French Doll tied a ribbon around Raggedy Cat's neck.

"Such a pretty little kitty needs a pretty little ribbon," Babette announced.

"How *cute!*" the other dolls exclaimed.

Raggedy Dog rolled over on his back. He stuck all four paws up in the air. But none of the dolls said, "Isn't that cute!"

They were all too busy saying how lovely Raggedy Cat looked with her pretty ribbon.

It had been like this ever since Marcella brought Raggedy Cat home from the toy store and Raggedy Dog had enough!

Raggedy Cat always played with Raggedy Dog's favorite toys.

"Isn't she *sweet!*" said the other dolls.

Raggedy Cat tagged along everywhere Raggedy Dog went.

"Isn't she *precious!*" said the other dolls.

And when Raggedy Cat curled up to sleep in Raggedy Dog's bed, they said, "Isn't that *adorable!*"

But Raggedy Dog didn't think so.

Raggedy Cat could tell that Raggedy Dog wasn't very happy with her. To make up for it, she gave him one of her favorite catnip toys.

"Isn't she *generous!*" said the other dolls.

"Humph!" thought Raggedy Dog. "Cats may love the smell of catnip, but dogs sure don't!"

He knew it would take days and days to get the catnip smell out of his bed.

Raggedy Dog started feeling so sorry for himself that he howled a sad little howl.

Raggedy Ann heard it and came right over.

"Look what I found," said Raggedy Ann, tossing a red rubber ball to him.

Raggedy Dog had thought his favorite red ball was lost.

He was very happy to see it again.

"I found it under the toy box," Raggedy Ann told him. Raggedy Dog wondered if Raggedy Cat had pushed it under the toy box!

And Raggedy Ann knew just what Raggedy Dog was thinking.

"I know how you feel, Raggedy Dog," she said. "Everyone makes a big fuss over Raggedy Cat. She's like a little baby, so cuddly and cute. But we still love you, too. You know that."

Raggedy Dog tossed his ball high into the air and caught it. He didn't think he wanted to hear what Raggedy Ann was saying.

"She follows you around and plays with your toys because she likes you so much," Raggedy Ann explained.

"Raggedy Cat wants to be your friend," Raggedy Ann told him. "She's young. You can teach her so many things. And you can help take care of her, too. You should feel special because she always wants to be with you."

Raggedy Dog curled up in his bed to think it over.
Soon he was asleep. But not for long!

A noise woke him up. It was the noise a cat makes playing with a red rubber ball—Raggedy Dog's red rubber ball!

"Come play with me!" meowed Raggedy Cat. And she dribbled the ball right under his nose.

Raggedy Cat had seen how much Raggedy Dog liked
to play with his ball.
She thought, "He'll like playing ball with me!"
He thought, "She's taken my ball again!"
And scrambling to his feet, Raggedy Dog chased
Raggedy Cat right out of the playroom!

He chased her down the back stairs and out the kitchen door . . .

through the backyard . . .

through the Deep Deep Woods . . .

and into Raggedy Land!

Raggedy Dog had been to Raggedy Land lots of times. But this was Raggedy Cat's first look at the clothespin fences, the thimble chimneys, and the pincushion trees. She thought it was a very wonderful place.

Before Raggedy Dog could stop her, she raced right to the top of a tall, tall pincushion tree to see more.

But when she looked down, she saw how very high the pincushion tree was. Suddenly, Raggedy Cat was terrified!

"Meow!" Raggedy Cat shouted as she clung to the tree. Raggedy Dog realized that she was too afraid to climb down by herself. Then he remembered what Raggedy Ann had told him about helping to take care of Raggedy Cat.

But how could he help? Dogs can't climb trees, and there were no low branches to jump on. If only Raggedy Andy were here. He'd know what to do.

"That's it!" thought Raggedy Dog. "I'll go get Raggedy Andy!" But as he turned to go, Raggedy Cat meowed louder than ever.

Raggedy Dog was afraid that if he left her alone, Raggedy Cat would fall out of the tree and hurt herself.

"I guess I'll just have to figure out a way to get you down myself," sighed Raggedy Dog.

He looked around. All he saw were more pincushion
trees. In fact, there was a whole field full of them.

That's when he noticed the pots. Raggedy Dog remembered that pincushion trees don't grow out of the ground. They are planted in pots instead. And pincushion trees come in all different sizes, from tall, tall trees way down to small, small trees.

If he pushed the different-sized trees into a row, he could make steps for Raggedy Cat to climb down.

Raggedy Dog worked fast. He knew it would soon be dark in Raggedy Land.

At last, panting and out of breath, Raggedy Dog was done.

Raggedy Cat looked at the steps Raggedy Dog had made with the treetops. Then she looked at Raggedy Dog, who was waiting for her below.

"Trust me, Raggedy Cat," Raggedy Dog called to her. "I'm trying to help you!"

Slowly and carefully, Raggedy Cat stepped down from treetop to treetop.

Raggedy Dog barked happily as she stepped off the last one.

"Gee, that was kind of scary," Raggedy Cat told him. "Thanks so much for helping me," she purred.

Raggedy Ann and Raggedy Andy arrived just as Raggedy Cat stepped safely onto the ground. They had come looking for their missing friends.

Raggedy Ann took the little cat in her arms, and
Raggedy Andy hugged Raggedy Dog. They saw how hard
Raggedy Dog had worked to save her. Together they all
hurried home to the playroom.

All the dolls in the playroom gave them a warm welcome. Babette set out teacups and a big pot of make-believe cocoa.

When Raggedy Andy told everybody how smart Raggedy Dog had been, they all cheered.

Raggedy Cat was very tired and sleepy from her journey. Soon she slipped away to her favorite spot—Raggedy Dog's bed.

Raggedy Dog found her there, but this time he didn't mind a bit.

He curled up beside Raggedy Cat and dropped his red rubber ball beside her.

Raggedy Ann saw them and smiled. "I think Raggedy Dog has a very special new friend," she whispered to Raggedy Andy.

Raggedy Dog opened one eye and peeped at Raggedy Cat. Raggedy Ann was right!

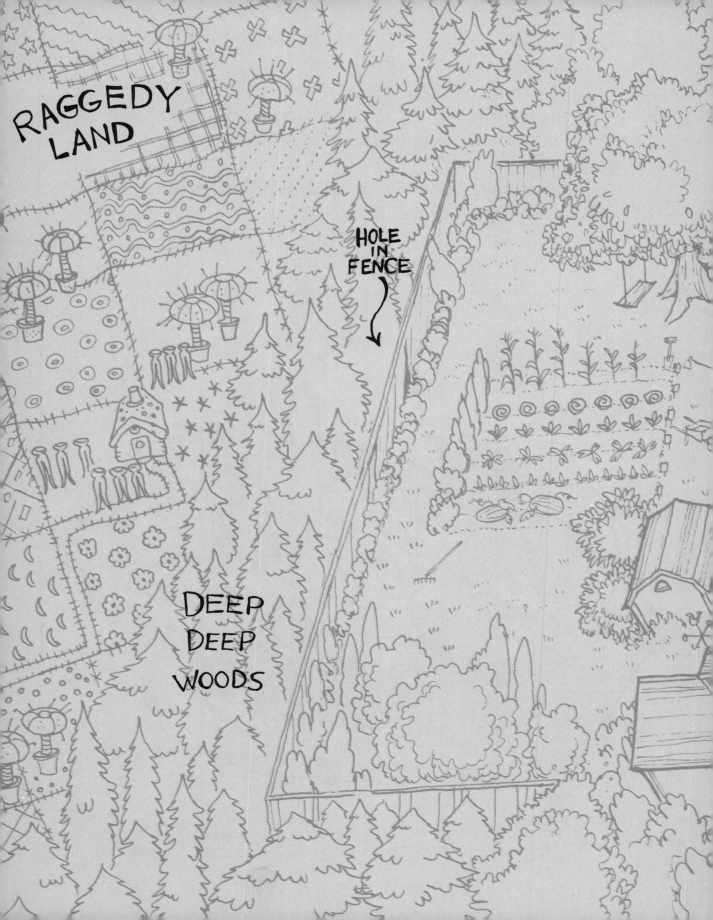